Never Let You GO

Patricia Storms

Sky Pony Press
New York

First published 2013 by Scholastic Canada Ltd.

First Sky Pony Press edition, 2018

Sky Pony Press books may be purchased in bulk at special discounts for sales
promotion, corporate gifts, fund-raising, or educational purposes. Special editions
can also be created to specifications. For details, contact the Special Sales
Department, Skyhorse Publishing, 307 West 36th Street, 11th Floor, New York,
NY 10018 or info@skyhorsepublishing.com.

Sky Pony® is a registered trademark of Skyhorse Publishing, Inc.®, a Delaware
corporation.

www.skyponypress.com

www.patriciastorms.com

10 9 8 7 6 5 4 3 2 1

Manufactured in China, July 2018
This product conforms to CPSIA 2008

The art in this book is a combination of traditional illustration usinga brush, India
ink, and charcoal pencil, combined with digital coloring using Photoshop.

Library of Congress Cataloging-in-Publication Data is available on file.

Cover design by Kate Gartner
Cover illustration by Patricia Storms

Print ISBN: 978-1-5107-3871-3
E-book ISBN: 978-1-5107-3872-0

For my Guido, of course. I'm a lucky penguin to have found you, and rest assured, I'll never let you go.

— P.S.

I love you,
little one.

I will care for you,

and treasure you always.

And I will never let you go.

Except when you need to
go to the bathroom.

And except when
it's time for lunch.

Or when you want to draw a picture.

But other than that,
little one . . .

I will never let you go.

Except when you have
to chase the stars.

And when you throw a tantrum.

Or need some
quiet time.

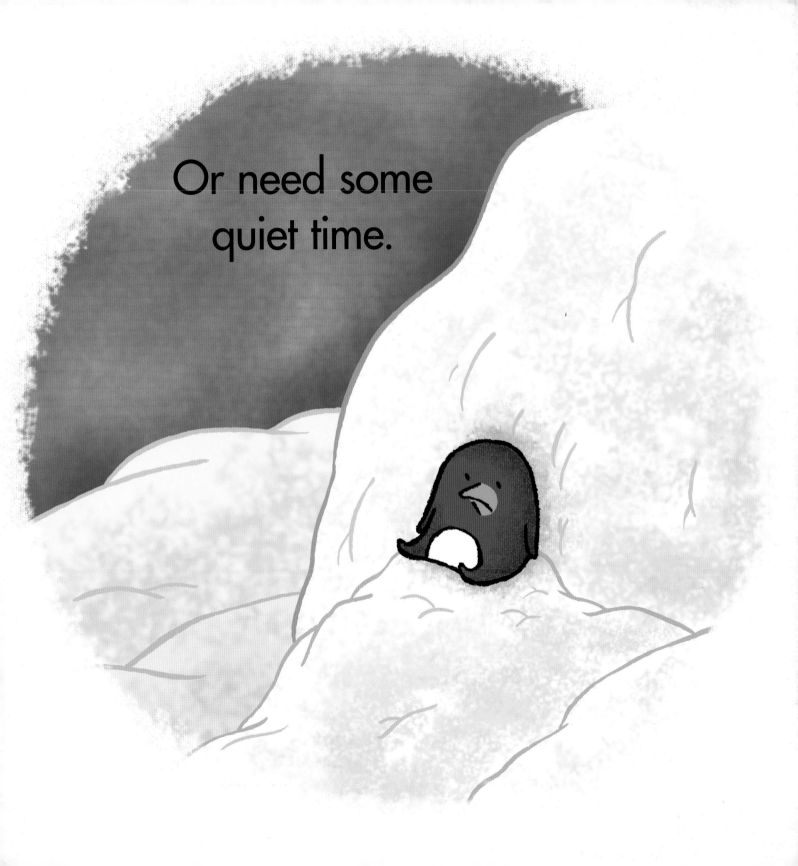

But other than that,
little one . . .

I will never let you go.

Except when you want
to play with your friends.

But other than that,
not-so-little one . . .

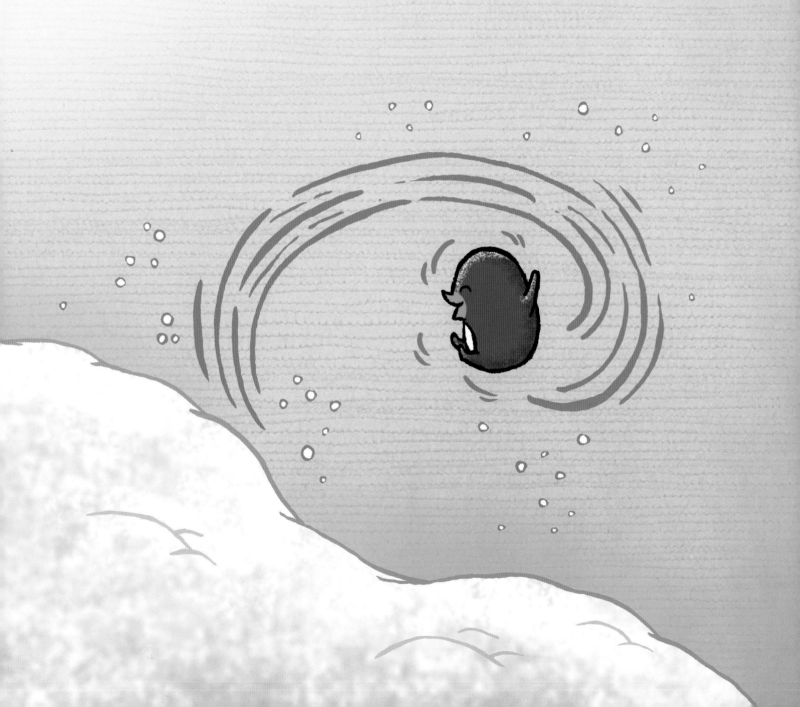

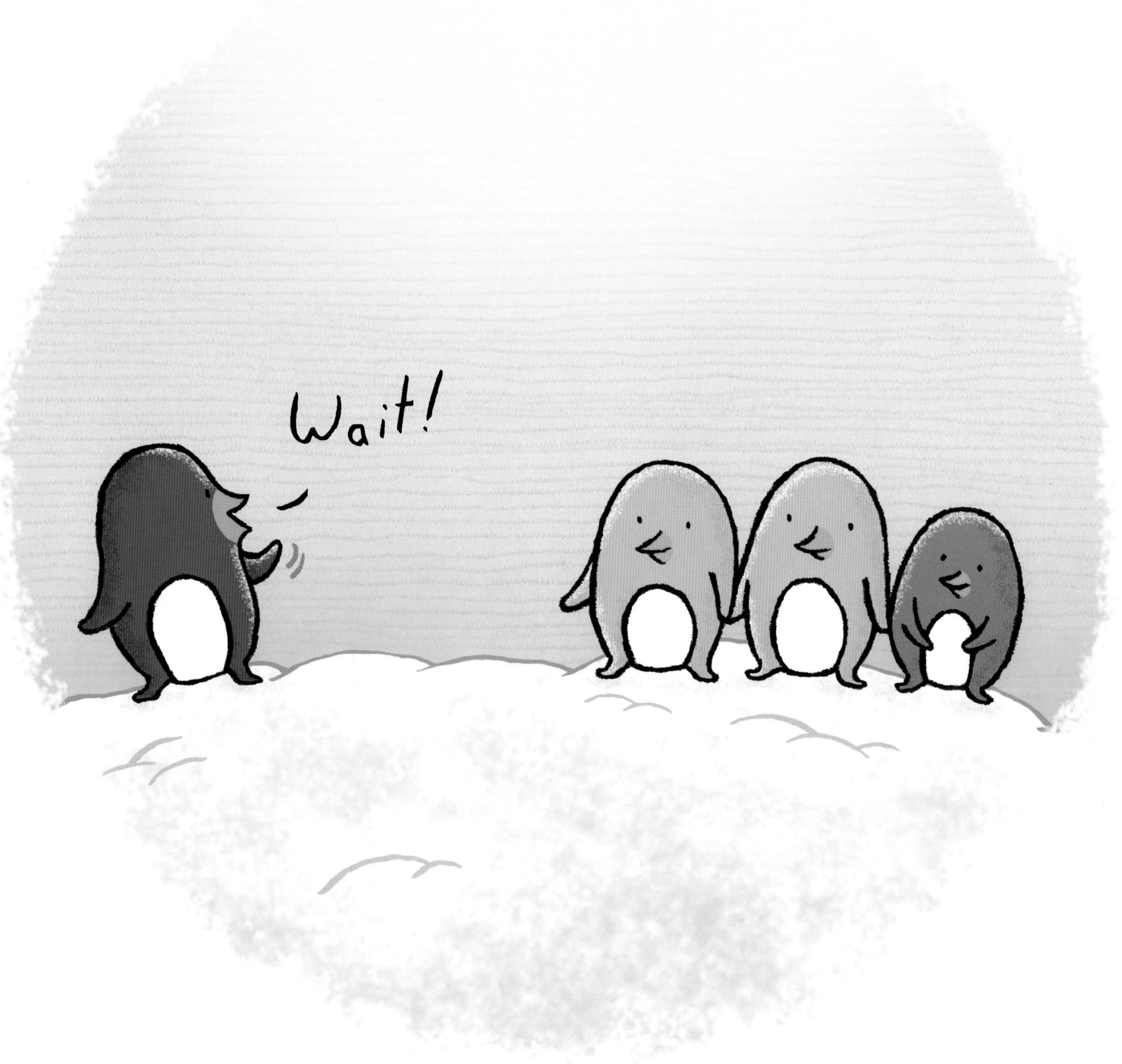
Wait!

I will never let you go.